I made this
book for:

_____

Love,

Alona

Once Upon a Potty

girl

Once Upon

girl

HarperFestival®

A Division of HarperCollinsPublishers

a Potty

Written and illustrated by Alona Frankel

Motto:

Panta Rei
(Everything Flows)

Heracleitus

To my sons, Ari and Michael

Dear Fellow-Parents,

Once Upon a Potty is best used as a companion volume to a child's new potty.
I wrote this book when my own child was toilet training to help him better
understand the process. My son was encouraged and excited by this story.
It motivated him to make the developmental leap from diaper to potty.

Potty talk has long been considered taboo in conversation – even between parent
and child. Thankfully, this attitude is changing, and children and parents are all
the happier for it. I believe that a frank and open approach to all bodily
functions is a good, healthy attitude toward child rearing. I have decided to use
"Wee-Wee" and "Poo-Poo" in this book, but I encourage you to read the story
with your child using words most suitable for you and your family.

Learning to use the potty is often a lengthy process, taxing the patience of both
parent and child. When success finally comes – and it should come in its own
good time without undue pressure or haste – it enhances the child's confidence
and pride. She has taken another step toward independence. She sat on the
potty as a little child and got up feeling ten feet tall.

It's one small step for mankind, but a giant one for your family.

Love,

Alona

Hello. I am Prudence's mother.
I'd like to tell you about Prudence
and her new potty.

This is Prudence.
Prudence is a little girl.

Just like you, Prudence has a body,
and this body has many nice and useful parts:

A head for thinking

Eyes for seeing

Ears for hearing

A mouth to talk
and eat with

Hands for playing

A pee-pee for
making
Wee-Wee

Legs for walking
and running

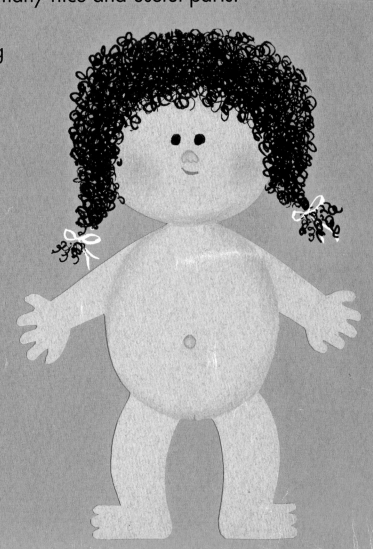

A bottom for sitting
and in it a little hole
for making Poo-Poo.

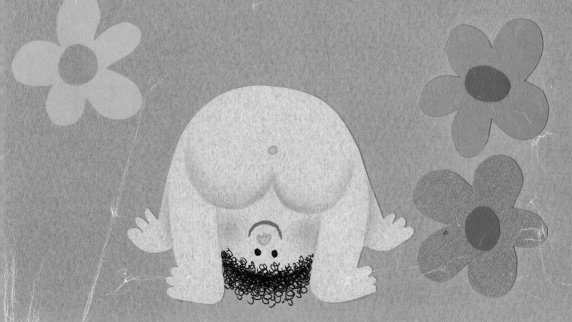

Ever since Prudence was born, she has been making
Wee-Wee and Poo-Poo into her diaper, and I,
her mother, have been changing her.
She was doing it when she was two days old.

She was doing it when she was two months old.

And here you see her,
still doing it,
and me, her mother,
changing her.

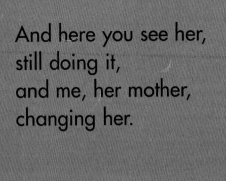

A clean diaper

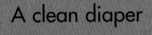

A diaper with
Wee-Wee and
Poo-Poo

A diaper with
Wee-Wee and
Poo-Poo

A clean
diaper

Until, one day, Prudence's grandmother
bought her a big present.

Prudence opened the box and found
a strange something inside.

Was it a hat?
No, it wasn't a hat.

Was it a milk bowl for the cat?
No, it wasn't a milk bowl
for the cat.

Was it a flowerpot?
No, it wasn't a flowerpot.

Was it a birdbath?
No, it wasn't a birdbath.

It was a potty, for sitting on and making
Wee-Wee and Poo-Poo into, instead of a diaper.
How wonderful!
Prudence was very happy.

She sat on her new potty
and sat and sat and sat and sat
and nothing came out,
neither Wee-Wee nor Poo-Poo.

Later on she made
both Wee-Wee and Poo-Poo
but not EXACTLY into the potty.

Afterwards she kept making Wee-Wee and Poo-Poo into her diaper and I, Prudence's mother, kept changing her.

Until, one day, when Prudence had a feeling
that Poo-Poo was ready to come out,
she ran to her potty and sat down on it.

She sat
and sat and sat and sat and sat
and sat and sat and sat and sat
and sat and sat and sat and sat
and sat and sat and sat and sat
and sat and sat and sat and sat
and sat and sat and sat and sat
and sat and sat and sat and sat
and sat and sat and sat and sat
and sat and sat and sat and sat
and sat and sat and sat and sat
and sat and sat and sat and sat
and sat and sat and sat and sat
and sat and sat and sat and sat
and sat and sat and sat and sat
and sat and sat and sat and sat
and sat and sat and sat and sat
and sat and sat and sat and sat
and sat and sat and sat and sat

and when she got up and looked into her potty
she saw all of her Wee-Wee and Poo-Poo
RIGHT INSIDE IT!

Prudence was very happy and proud
and came to show me her full potty
and I, Prudence's mother, was also
very happy, and proud of Prudence.

And then the two of us,
I, Prudence's mother, and Prudence,
carried the potty to the bathroom
and emptied it into the toilet.

"Bye-bye, Wee-Wee.
Bye-bye, Poo-Poo,"
said Prudence.

And now she likes
her potty even more
and uses it every time.

Alona Frankel
is the author and illustrator
of over thirty titles for children.
She is the recipient of numerous
awards, and her books and art
are seen all around the world.
Ms. Frankel lives in Tel Aviv, Israel.

Find out more about Alona
on the internet at:
www.alonafrankel.com

Join Joshua and Prudence, the adorable
Once Upon a Potty characters, in a
new series of charming adventures.

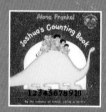

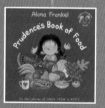